For Camille
S.R.

Reycraft Books
55 Fifth Avenue
New York, NY 10003

Reycraftbooks.com

Reycraft Books is a trade imprint and trademark of Newmark Learning, LLC.

© HongFei Publishing Co., Ltd, 2014
This edition is published by arrangement with HongFei Publishing Co., Ltd. , through Syllables Agency.
Translated from French by Julien Yeh.

Educators and Librarians: Our books may be purchased in bulk for promotional, educational, or business use. Please
contact sales@reycraftbooks.com.

This is a work of fiction. Names, characters, places, dialogue, and incidents described either are the product of the author's
imagination or are used fictitiously. Any resemblance to actual persons, living or dead, is entirely coincidental.

Sale of this book without a front cover or jacket may be unauthorized. If this book is coverless, it may have been reported
to the publisher as "unsold or destroyed" and may have deprived the author and publisher of payment.

Library of Congress Control Number: 2020909964

ISBN: 978-1-4788-7031-9

Printed in Dongguan, China. 8557/0820/17296

10 9 8 7 6 5 4 3 2 1

First Edition Hardcover published by Reycraft Books 2020

Reycraft Books and Newmark Learning, LLC, support diversity and
the First Amendment, and celebrate the right to read.

IT'S
NOT VERY
COMPLICATED

A story written and illustrated by

Samuel RIBEYRON

Louise is my neighbor.

Our homes face each other, so we meet often.

With Louise, I don't talk much.

We exchange looks, and we draw.

We draw trees on the ground with big colored chalk,
because our street is very small and not very pretty.
We give them big trunks, long branches, and leaves of all colors.

Sometimes a car passes and rolls over our forest.

Louise loves to draw my head peeking out of the leaves.

It's funny. She often gives me a round head,

with a big nose and a lot of hair.

Yesterday, while drawing, Louise asked me what I have inside my head.

Good question...

But I didn't know what to say to her.

So I wanted to see what really was inside my head.

It's not very complicated.

I just need to open it the right way.

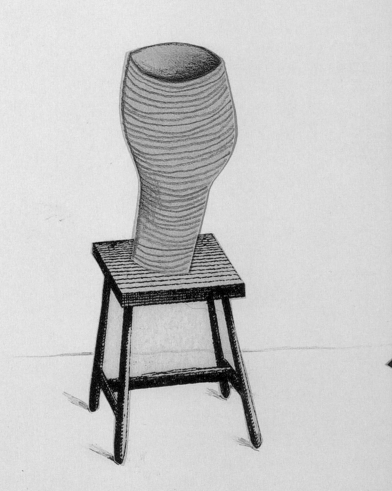

And that is how I discovered...

a forest!

A quiet
forest.

A secret forest.

A shy forest.

A dark forest.

A sweet
forest.

A mysterious
forest.

And then, in a corner,

the forest on our street.

I gently closed my head,
and stood there, without moving.
I needed to tell all of this to Louise.

But Louise was gone. Forever.

And I was left alone with my colored chalk.

When the rain washed the trees off our street,

I didn't even cry.

What if I don't have a heart?

So, I went to see...
to check.

It's not very complicated.
I just need to open it the right way.

And there, I found...

Louise.

Samuel RIBEYRON is a graduate of the Émile-Cohl school in France and has been inspired by his numerous trips, notably to China and Japan. He writes and illustrates books for children and directs animated films.

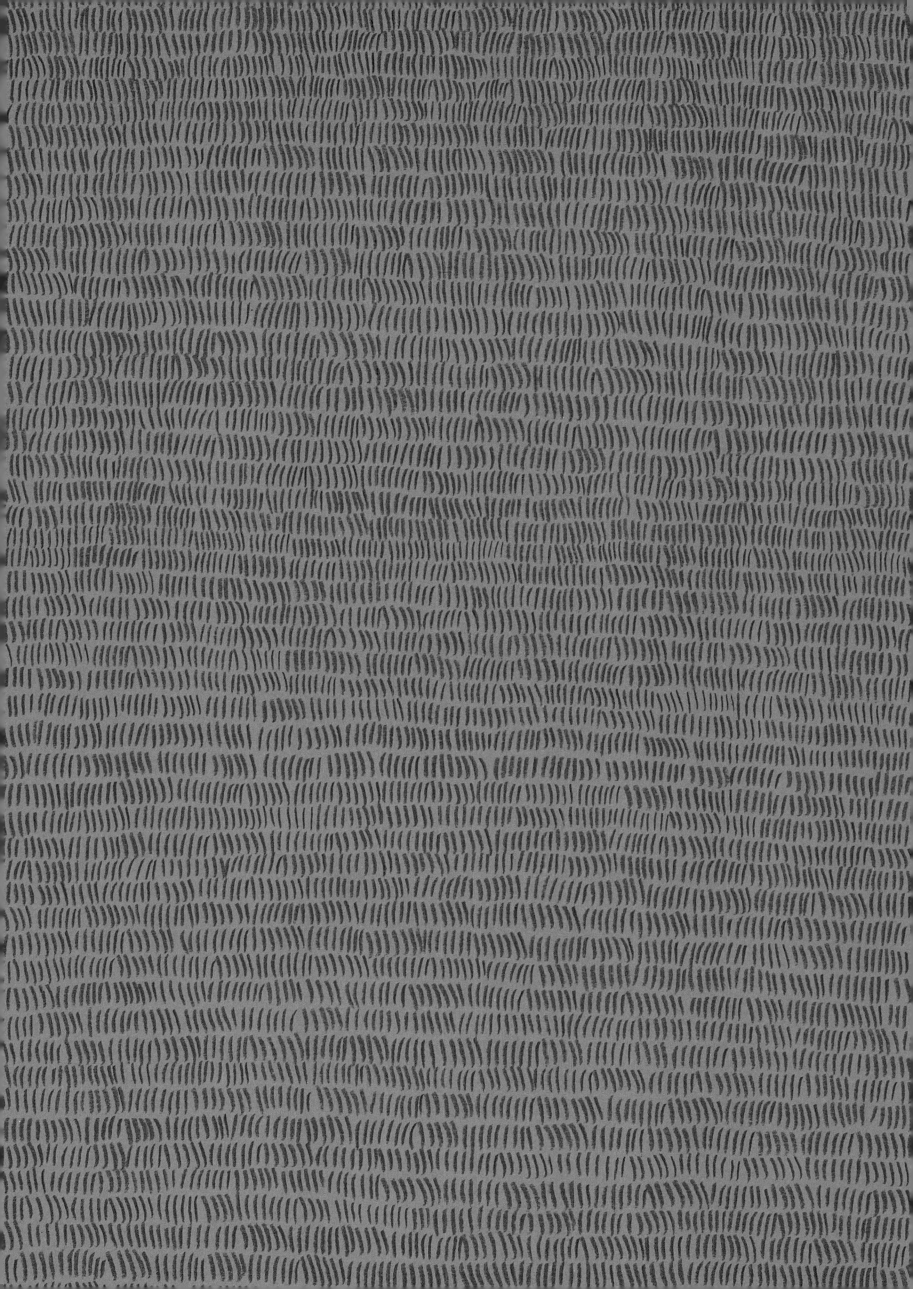

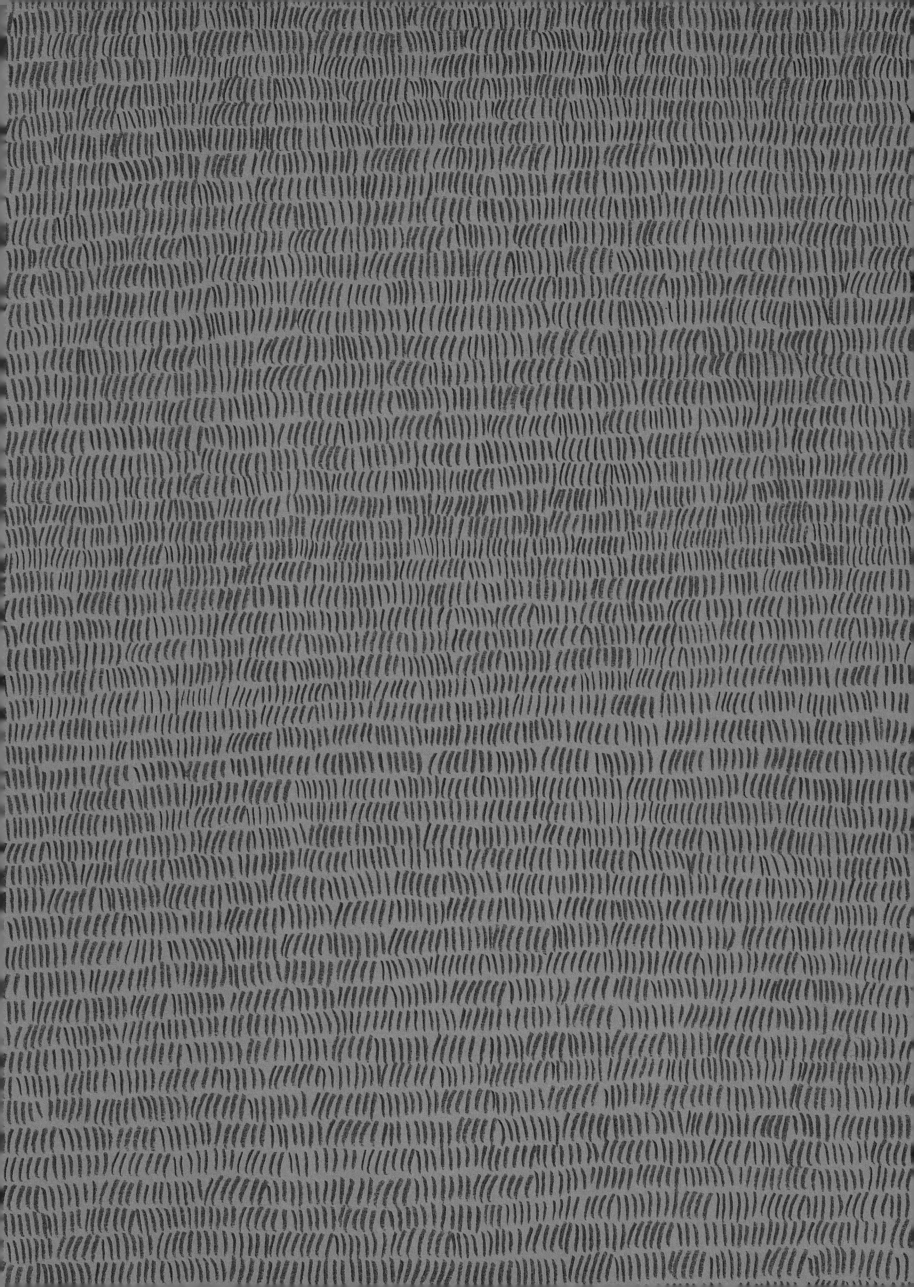